MW00945357

THAT LITTLE THING

THAT LITTLE THING

A Life Changing Story

JEAN MARIE DESIR

XULON PRESS ELITE

Xulon Press Elite
2301 Lucien Way #415
Maitland, FL 32751
407.339.4217
www.xulonpress.com

© 2021 by Jean Marie Desir

All rights reserved solely by the author. The author guarantees all contents are original and do not infringe upon the legal rights of any other person or work. No part of this book may be reproduced in any form without the permission of the author. The views expressed in this book are not necessarily those of the publisher.

Unless otherwise indicated, Scripture quotations taken from the King James Version (KJV) – *public domain.*

Scripture quotations taken from the New King James Version (NKJV). Copyright © 1982 by Thomas Nelson, Inc. Used by permission. All rights reserved.

Scripture quotations taken from the English Standard Version (ESV). Copyright © 2001 by Crossway, a publishing ministry of Good News Publishers. Used by permission. All rights reserved.

Scripture quotations taken from the Holy Bible, New International Version (NIV). Copyright © 1973, 1978, 1984, 2011 by Biblica, Inc.™. Used by permission. All rights reserved.

Paperback ISBN-13: 978-1-6628-1078-7

Ebook ISBN-13: 978-1-6628-1079-4

This book is dedicated to my beautiful and elegant mother,
Gesila Marie Desir.
You are the greatest example of a godly woman.
You always have been and always will be my greatest inspiration.
I thank you very much.

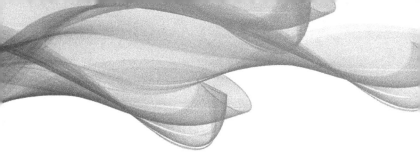

Contents

Acknowledgments

I think my good friend and bestselling author Rene Godefroy said it best: "It is virtually impossible for me to mention all the people who have directly or indirectly provided me with some kind of assistance." But I promise that I will do my best.

First and foremost, I would like to thank God for His never-ending grace and mercy toward me.

I'm eternally grateful to my second mother, Nadie Celestin (Manmie Dusseck). She taught me discipline, manners, respect and so much more.

Thank you so much Tatie Marie-Rose and Micheline Celestin.

Next, a special thanks to my very first mentor and editor Eveline Saillant for your dedication, patience, and guidance with this book. Eveline (La lune), I am so grateful to you for being there any time I have needed your input. I appreciate you coaching me through the entire process. I value your friendship.

I would also like to thank the following people:

To Ossepha Desir, my wife. Thanks for your ongoing support and encouragement during this project.

To my sisters Silviana, Kettly, Fabienne, Regine, and my brothers Eric, Jean Richard, Emmanuel, and Jean Pierre who never wavered in their love and support. I love you so much, guys!

To my children, nephews, nieces, and all the little girls and boys in the world. I dedicate this book to you.

I especially want to thank the individuals who helped make this happen. Complete thanks go to Jerlyn Goodwin, Karen Garner, Pastor Jean Richard Desir, and Pastor Kelissa G. Delva.

I want to thank my friend, my mentor, bestselling author Rene Godefroy, for all your support and your encouraging words.

Marlie, Marie-Danielle, Johanna, Marc, Camille, Scott, Sauveur Moise Desir, Madame Maxene, Manmie Douce, The Durocher family, Manmie Jo, Linda Vital, Sophie Casimir, Stephanie and Jude Cassagnol, Carline Germain, Nathalie Janvier, Darline Leontus, Ajajou, Manmie Rolandia, Manou, Patrick Pierre-fils, Monica, Beverly, Tim Wallace, David Loftis, Ken Johnson, Charles William, Ronald McCoy, Princess Tondalaya of North Carolina, Sandra Morris, Betsy, Debbie, Alex Mode, Sabrina Baxter, Chantal Viellard, Trudi, my angel, Eldaa, Les Sardonyx, Martine Barthelemy, Magalie Delizin and

ACKNOWLEDGMENTS

Gabie Desir, thank you for your support and encouragement through the rough times.

A special thanks to my photographer Jakeem Smith (Jayproductions Agency)

I would like to include a special word of thanks and gratitude to my other editors. Their support and dedication to helping spread this message worldwide is invaluable. I could not have done it without you.

Finally, there are no words to express my appreciation to my extended family on Facebook, Instagram, Twitter, and WhatsApp. Every day, your stories inspire me to continue writing. I hope that together we can do our part in changing the world.

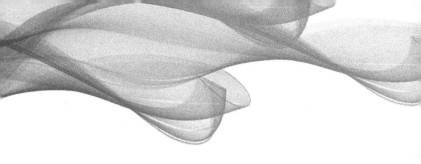

Foreword

*H*aving known Jean Marie for many years, I can speak of a brother with a deep love of Christ. It shines through his countenance. Jean Marie's joy is infectious, and it is rare to see him without a smile on his face. His love and gratitude for Jesus Christ is what compels him to share his faith and testimony with everyone. As a gifted vocalist, Jean Marie shares his gift of music to uplift and inspire congregations and audiences here and abroad. And, he is always proclaiming the divinity of Jesus Christ.

In this book are gospel principles that will resonate with readers, young and old. The characters face real issues that many of us face each day. Though the characters are fictional, their trials and experiences offer hope and inspiration. Through a perspective of faith, you will see how God works miracles in what we see as hopeless situations.

It is my heartfelt wish that this book would inspire individuals and families; that they would embrace this earthly journey with grateful hearts; that all would recognize the significance of our bodies being the temples wherein our spirits dwell. May we follow the Shepherd who knows the way and who is the way.

It is my deepest hope that the powerful examples of faith, repentance, and redemption will help us remember our worth in the eyes of God; that all who have faith in Christ, and act upon it, will receive an abundance of the blessings discussed herein.

Andrea Davis

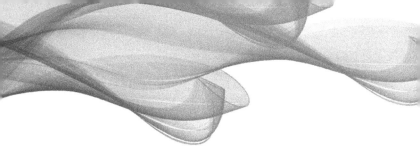

Introduction

*I*n 2005, I took a college course in public speaking. At the end of the class, Professor Susan Wallace asked us to prepare and deliver an oral presentation that was both captivating and informative.

Ninety percent of the students in this class were female, with roughly sixty-five percent being a parent to one or more children. The youngest student was probably in her twenties.

As the presentation began, each student went up in front of the class and gave his or her best presentation. When Professor Wallace introduced me, I took several deep breaths to settle my nerves and then got out of my chair. As my muscles tensed, my heart began to beat very fast—so hard it felt like someone knocked the breath out of me.

As I moved closer to the lectern, I heard my fellow classmates say "You can do it, Jean. Come on. Go ahead and do your thing!" Slowly, I regained my confidence. I was getting ready to talk about a very sensitive subject.

Thoughts raced through my mind. I had prepared my material and considered every detail as my professor suggested—or so I thought at the time.

When I approached the lectern, I counted to ten before I spoke, as Professor Wallace had advised. At home, I had already practiced my speech many times out loud.

I had used a mirror to have an idea of how I looked when speaking to an audience. I also practiced making eye contact with the class. And, as Professor Wallace had instructed, I stood in the corner of my study room. I did this to get an idea of how my voice carried throughout the room. I used a tape recorder, which helped me playback the speech to check my accent. My native languages are Creole and French, and I wanted to make sure I pronounced each word with clarity.

I looked at the audience and suddenly felt more confident and in control, at least for a few seconds. To begin, I thanked my professor for her introduction and acknowledged my classmates.

Unfortunately, during my preparations, I had failed to practice in front of someone for feedback. Well, that was a huge mistake of mine.

When I announced my speech's title and explained what it meant, the class erupted into total chaos. I was trying to give a speech about female sexuality. I had wanted to impart a message of empowerment, dignity, and respect toward young women. I wanted to encourage them not only to hold to biblical values but to see how doing so would be to their advantage.

Instead, everything came out wrong. The way I framed the message was deeply offensive to many young women in the class. I take full responsibility for this.

But at the time, I did not understand the ladies' anger. I felt hurt and attacked by their reaction having tried to do something good. I realize now that most of my classmates felt demeaned by the way I presented the message.

This book represents my best attempt to correct myself and the message I intended to convey. My hope is my mistakes and pain will lead to someone else's gain.

This book is not a novel, but it does use fictional illustrations to help communicate the message I believe God has given to me. My goal is to help young women understand how powerful they are in shaping our society. I want to help them use that power the way God intends, for their good, the good of their families, and the good of our world.

In a healthy and loving way, I want to help all of us understand and address the following problems:

- Why our children are having sex at an early stage
- Why over a million teenage girls are getting pregnant every year

- Why we have more single parents than ever before
- Why we are failing to communicate with our children to prepare them for a better future
- How to heal from past sins and mistakes

Romans 3:23 says, "For all have sinned, and come short of the glory of God." (KJV) We all make mistakes. God is using an imperfect person like me, the lowest of the low, to convey His message. The messages in this book aren't just for others. They are for me as well. As I was working on this book, God revealed things that made me stop and think about my life and mistakes throughout my adult life.

As a society, we have made many collective mistakes. Together, we can learn from our experiences. We can communicate the importance of biblical values to our children, families, and friends.

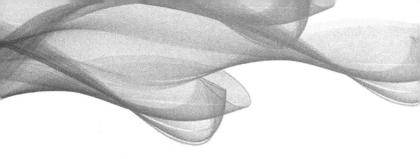

Chapter 1

Graduation Day

*D*aniel and Jackie are among thousands who will attend high school graduation where their daughter, Ananie, now 18 years old, is about to graduate high school. They can recall her graduations from preschool, elementary, and middle school. Joy and excitement fill them each time Ananie achieves the next level in her life.

But this is the big one. The one after which they will send her out into the world to be a young adult woman, making her own choices. They hope they've done well. They hope she won't make the same mistakes they made in life.

Family and friends are coming from all over to show their appreciation and support, and Jackie's house is frantic with activity.

Getting Ready

"Ananie, honey! You need to be a little bit faster," Jackie shouted with love. "Your dad will be here any moment."

"Mom, I was ready a long time ago," Ananie replied sarcastically, "and by the way, Auntie Darline called a while ago. By the grace of God, she and her aunties had a safe flight from Haiti. They are spending some time with Uncle Jean-Richard. They will meet us at the ceremony."

"Very well," Jackie said with relief.

Ananie continued, "Nathalie will come straight from the airport."

"Great!" yelled Jackie as she continued to scramble around the house.

The doorbell rang, as Jackie finished applying some light makeup, she yelled out for Ananie to get the door. Ananie scurried downstairs and looked through the eyehole of the front door to see who was there. It was Daniel, her father. She opened the door and jumped into his arms, filled with joy and happiness. "Hi, Daddy!" she shouted.

"There's my beautiful princess. How are you?" Daniel said with much contentment.

"I'm well, Daddy. How are you?" she replied.

"Well, look at me, can't you see your daddy is fine?"

He hugged her tight and kissed her cheek again and again. "Wow, you look great," he said as he continued to hold her.

Ananie was indeed a beautiful young lady, unique and exotic like her mother, Jackie. She thanked her dad for the compliment.

Daniel continued, "Ananie, there are no words that can express my happiness for you. I am so proud of your great achievement. From the bottom of my heart, I am extremely proud of you, princess, and I will be there for you for as long you need me." Ananie was proud and grateful for her dad's gratitude.

Daniel looked at his watch and said to Ananie, "Ok, it's almost time to leave now. Remember, you should be at the place one hour before the ceremony."

Ananie nodded her head in agreement.

"Where's your mother?" he asked with anticipation.

"She's getting ready. Mom! Daddy is here!" Ananie shouted.

"Yes, I'm coming. Do you have everything?" Jackie asked.

"Yes, Mother, let me get my purse," Ananie replied.

When Jackie came out, she saw Daniel in the living room, his hand behind his back, walking back and forth. Jackie stared at Daniel, wearing a dark suit with a light blue shirt and no tie. It suited him very well. She looked at him like it was years since they had seen each other. *Wow! He looks very handsome* she thought to herself.

"Hey, Daniel. How are you?" she said, taking a deep breath.

"I'm well, thank you, Jackie," Daniel replied, as he walked toward her and kissed her forehead. Jackie closed her eyes to enjoy that rare and precious moment.

"How are you?" Daniel hit back.

"I...I'm fantastic. Thank you," she replied, distracted. Her mind went back sixteen years prior—before their separation. She remembered how everything used to be so wonderful.

"Jackie. Jackie? Jackie!" Daniel said, trying to get her attention.

"Oh, yes, sorry," she said, coming back to earth.

"Is everything okay?" Daniel asked with concern.

"Yes, yes. I'm great," she said, trying to convince herself that everything was okay.

"By the way, you look beautiful!" Daniel said.

"Me?" Jackie replied with surprise.

Daniel checked around and said, "You're the only one here, right?"

"Well, thank you, Daniel. Thank you. That's— that's so sweet of you. I appreciate it," she replied with mixed feelings.

It had been a while since someone reminded her how beautiful she was, at least the right person. She would give anything in the world to be in his arms again because Daniel is the only man she has ever loved. She still does, but *it's a dream, wishful thinking,* she tells herself.

"You still wear that cologne, huh?" Jackie said, trying to get outside of her own mind.

"Oh yes, I like it," Daniel replied with a half-smile. "That was one of the first gifts you gave me."

Jackie scratched her head, "Yes, that's true. Wow— you still remember," she said with a slight blush.

"Can I fix your shirt for you?" Jackie asked, finding a way to change the subject again.

"Sure! Thank you," Daniel said. "Jackie?"

"Yes, Daniel?"

"How's your mom?"

"She's fine. Thank you for asking. She'll meet us at the auditorium. How's your mother?" Jackie asked.

"She's great too. Thank you."

Daniel stood in front of Jackie. He tried to avoid making eye contact, but he couldn't resist their entire exchange. They shared a few glances while continuing their small talk and making each other laugh for a few more minutes.

A Daughter's Longing

Ananie walked to the living room and saw her parents having a pleasant conversation. She enjoyed the moment. She appreciated the way they looked at each other. She could feel there was once a connection between them. Her parents have always refused to tell her what happened sixteen years ago. Still, she hoped that somehow, someday, both of her parents would share the same roof again.

Ananie couldn't recall the last time she witnessed her parents in the house together. It didn't happen often. Besides that, they celebrated her birthday and other events apart. It was killing her inside. As Ananie enjoyed the moment, Daniel excitedly said, "It's time. Let's go!"

The Ceremony

The auditorium was full as they arrived at the ceremony. A sense of excitement and joy was in the air. Ananie joined the other students behind the podium. In the meantime, Daniel and Jackie sat with other parents and friends.

Although Daniel and Jackie had separated a while ago, the two families got along pretty well. They had all gathered here to support Ananie and celebrate her great achievement.

All the students wore their graduation caps and gowns and sat down in alphabetical order. After all the recognitions, Principal Stephanie called out each student.

When the principal called Ananie, she walked across the stage. She paused to shake hands with the vice-principal, who handed Ananie her diploma. She posed for a quick picture as she walked off the stage with a beaming smile. She looked over at her parents and friends. They were all very proud and made a passionate display of support for Ananie.

In a little while, it was time for the keynote speaker. Mayor Frantz Darius came and approached the podium with a message of hope and encouragement:

Principal Stephanie, members of the school board, teachers, parents, friends, and fellow graduates:

It is an honor to speak to all of you today at the high school where I learned so much about life, the world, and myself.

In the United States, an average of 7000 students drop out of high school every single day of the year.[1] Too many teenagers end up in gangs, pregnant, or on drugs. Too many youths end up in jail or have a record to follow them for the rest of their life. Amidst this backdrop, you, students, deserve to be happy, and your parents deserve to be proud.

According to the Department of Justice, in 2013, there were 1.57 million people in federal and state prisons. This number does not even include the local and county jails. Prisoners also tend to be less educated; the average state prisoner has a tenth-grade education, and about seventy percent have not completed high school.

But you have overcome many obstacles. Instead, you have chosen the good path—you have achieved despite various challenges, hard work, education, blessings, and prosperity for yourselves and future generations. It is our desire and our hope for this graduating class, that you will be among those self-assured enough to make personal sacrifices for what is right and just. Therefore, be passionate. Be strong. Be courageous.

If you remember these things, you will continue to make us proud of you. You will make your parents continually proud, and I dare say, you will greatly impact and benefit your country, and indeed the whole world, with the unique treasures you will give to it. So today, I urge each one of you graduates to embrace the opportunity before you. Take what you have learned and put it to good use. Congratulations, and may the Lord continue to bless you all!

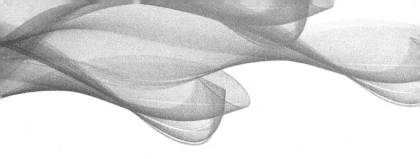

Chapter 2
The Get-Together

*A*fter the ceremony, Ananie's family and friends went to a nearby restaurant to celebrate. After several hours of quality interaction, everyone congratulated her one last time. Some of them gave her gifts, money, or cards.

It was time to go home since it was getting late, and some of them had early flights the next morning. Most everyone said their final goodbyes to Ananie and her parents and then left. Daniel, Jackie, and Ananie got to spend some more time together, talking and laughing.

Daniel, feeling delighted, decided to say a few words. "Ananie, my love, today your mom and I want to take this opportunity once again...and again..." he paused and smiled, "and again...and again to tell you how proud and honored we are to be your parents."

Jackie looked at Daniel and Ananie, and interjected, "Yes, indeed! Words cannot express our love and satisfaction toward you. You've been a good kid throughout your life."

Daniel, always trying to joke around, came back with a sarcastic face. "What? Are you sure she's always been good? You forgot about all the dirty diapers and the sleepless nights." They all laughed, and Daniel continued, "But it was worth it, no doubt about that. You make us very happy, Ananie."

Jackie responded "Yes, you make us very proud."

"Awww! Thank you, Mother, Dad." With tears welling up in her eyes and her voice getting a bit tight, she continued, "I am so blessed and fortunate to have both of you as my parents. You've taught me so many things since I was a baby until now. Sometimes I tested you guys on purpose. I wanted some freedom—you know—to do what I thought was right at that time. But you guys made me understand—sometimes the hard way—the importance of obedience and what was and is right for me.

Ananie paused for a moment and then went on, "Now I am honestly beginning to realize how your tough love paid off. It was not because you hated me or you just enjoyed being tough on me, but instead, you wanted to prepare me for a better tomorrow. I will forever be grateful for your presence in my life. I am a much better human being because of you guys. I thank you from the bottom of my heart," she concluded.

Daniel and Jackie, both very emotional and feeling honored, replied together, "You are very welcome!"

Daniel continued, "And because you have done a great job and also accomplished the goals of moving on to the next stage, not only academically but also of your life..." At that point, Daniel paused to let Jackie join in. Jackie chimed in and said, "We want to give you a little present to commemorate your advancement to the next level of school and life." Jackie then reached in her bag and pulled out a wrapped gift.

Ananie looked shocked. "Daddy! Mom!"

"What?" Daniel asked, with a sly shrug.

"What is it?" Ananie said.

"Well, why don't you open it?" Daniel replied with a half-smile.

From time to time, he looked at Jackie. She was so happy to be with her family—to have a feeling of wholeness—although it was only for a short moment. She tried to enjoy every moment of it. She hung onto the thought that all of them could just go home together, but she knew it was only wishful thinking.

Ananie opened her gift. It was a laptop and a ticket to go to Labadie, a gorgeous resort on the east side of Haiti. She was so happy. She didn't know what to do or how to react. First, she got up and ran to her father and hugged him tightly. Then she ran to her mother to show her appreciation with another big hug.

Ananie began to speak with some emotion, "Mom, Dad, one more thing—I have to let it out."

"Okay," Daniel replied.

Jackie encouraged her and said, "Go for it, honey."

"Since I was a little girl, I started learning good values from you guys. You planned and devoted time to parenting me. You guys made the development of my character your top priority, and you made sacrifices to spend more of your day caring for me. Dad, even though you were not always at home, I know—I know you told me that we won't talk about whatever happened to you and Mom, at least not for now. That's fine."

Ananie became a bit uncomfortable and started to ramble, "But although you weren't there all the time, I still felt your presence with me. Dad, I did. You were always taking care of me so that Mom could have time for herself, and you did the same for her. I can still hear your deep voice in my head, 'Ananie, what did I tell you to do when you finished playing with your toys?'"

"And I answered, 'To put them in their respective places, Daddy.' And then you would ask, 'Okay then, why don't you put them in their respective places?' Sometimes I refused to pick up my toys, or fix my bed, or forgot to say please or thank you. Other times I refused to follow the rules, you know the rule sheet you put at the bathroom door or the refrigerator door?"

"What was it again?" Daniel replied.

"You know the good hygiene thing," Ananie hit back, "like brushing and flossing my teeth, taking baths or showers, and putting on deodorant and fresh clothes after bathing—all the good stuff."

Daniel smiled and joked, "Oh, now it is the good stuff, huh?"

"Yes, that's true," she responded with a blush. "And if I refused, you came toward me in a gentle but firm manner and told me, 'You will do as you are told, or you will pay the consequences.' And sometimes I learned the very hard way. But one of the many things I admired dearly from you and my mother—"

Jackie, urging Ananie to speak her mind, asked, "What is it?"

Ananie took a few seconds to get their undivided attention. "You always told me the reason why you didn't want me to do something. And most of the time, the reason you gave helped me better understand and respect your wishes."

"That is good. That is good to hear," Daniel said.

Ananie continued, "I always noticed, Dad, how you respect Mom and how she speaks to you with respect. I always wonder why you are not under the same roof. But, well, that is Mom's and your secret."

Daniel and Jackie froze.

Everyone sat in silence for a moment.

Then Ananie broke the awkwardness and saved the night by adding, "Yet I still feel blessed and loved by you two. Thank you. You guys are good parents.

You taught me good values, respect, care, courtesy, obedience, and love."

Jackie tried to lighten the mood. "How about understanding?"

Ananie agreed, "Yes, Mom! Understanding, and so much more."

They all laughed before Ananie hugged her parents one last time.

"Thank you, love!" Daniel said. "I want you to know, that not only am I your father and Jackie your mother, but we are your friends. We promise you that we will always listen to you when you come to us. We may not tell you what you want to hear all the time, but we will tell you what is good for you and your future. Please, do not hesitate to call me or speak to your mom at any time, day or night. If I cannot talk to you right away, I will make time for you."

"Thank you," Ananie said.

Everyone said their goodbyes, and afterward, Daniel dropped Jackie and Ananie off at home. Ananie said her last goodbye of the night to Daniel before taking off to her room.

Jackie felt a little shy in front of Daniel and then spoke up, "Well, we made it. It was a long journey, but, by the grace of God, we did it."

Daniel responded with confidence, "Yes, indeed, we did it. And you know what? You play a major role, Jackie, in our daughter's life. I am very aware that I was not there much of the time—I mean in the same house. Most nights, you had to be Mom and Dad. From the bottom of my heart, thank you! You are a great mother, and I'm really proud of you."

Jackie felt honored, and said, "Thank you, Daniel. That means a lot to me. I really appreciate that."

Daniel smiled and said, "I need to get home, Jackie. Do you need anything before I go?"

Jackie wanted to say, *Let's start all over again. I have missed you in my life. I've been alone and without a man for the last sixteen years. I need love. Stay for tonight and make me feel like a woman again. I miss you with my whole heart. I miss your lips, your kiss, the way you look at me, and your laugh.*

"Jackie, Jackie?" Daniel tried to get her attention.

She snapped back into the moment and replied, "No, I'm good. Thank you."

"Okay, take care, and have a blessed night."

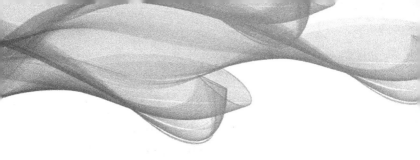

Chapter 3

The Meeting

A little later that night, Ananie came down-stairs. She saw her mother, Jackie, standing on the balcony. As she came closer, she noticed tears flowing down Jackie's eyes. Ananie approached Jackie with concern and asked, "Mom. Mom? What's wrong? Why are you crying?"

Jackie shook her head in denial and insisted, "It's okay, honey, I—I'm fine." She hugged Ananie tightly.

Ananie countered, "No, Mom!" She pushed Jackie back just a bit and snapped, "It's not okay, Mother! You've been like this for years. You've tried to hide it from me for so long, and I think it's time to tell me what's bothering you. I'm really concerned about you. Is it because of Dad? What happened? Please tell me."

Jackie slowly took Ananie's hand, walked with her to the living room, and sat down. She took her time, looked at her, and smiled. Jackie touched her face and hair. Then stood up and began to pace a little. "Ananie, it's a long story," she said.

Ananie was unrelenting. "I won't sleep tonight anyway," she said.

Jackie wiped her face, took a deep breath, and then began an explanation that was many years overdue. "Your father was the best thing that ever happened to me. There was nobody I trusted more than him. He was sweet, funny, and caring. He was such a gentleman, and he still is."

Jackie smiled at the thought of pleasant memories coming to her mind. "The beauty of our relationship was, well, the way we met was like magic, almost like God destined us to meet each other that day. I certainly did not see it coming. Your father and I? Together? Oh no, I didn't see it coming, even after I had first met him. My life was such a mess before I met your father, but let me get to the story.

"It was twenty-two years ago at a singles ministry retreat. People came from all over the United States to the Georgia Dome in Atlanta.

"You can imagine the place was overflowing with all kinds of young people. There were Blacks, Whites, Asians, Latinos, Caribbeans, Africans, and Europeans. I mean all races, full of life and energy. And it seemed they all wanted to be there. The praise teams and musicians were well prepared. I could feel the Holy Spirit in that place."

Jackie felt much better now, far more relaxed and peaceful. Ananie stayed quiet and very attentive. She had been waiting for that story for a long time. She really wanted to understand what happened between her parents.

Jackie continued, "I still remember the last sermon Pastor Dennis preached that weekend. The title was 'How to Start the Right Way in Relationships.' One day, I'll tell you more about that sermon.

"At the end of his message, Pastor Dennis prayed and gave an altar call. Young people from all over the Dome, including me, were walking down the aisle toward the stage. Pastor Dennis asked everyone to take our neighbor's hand and pray together. Suddenly, someone grabbed my hand, and when I looked up, it was a handsome young gentleman. He smiled at me. I have to tell you, Ananie, he had a beautiful smile, and I returned the favor. I looked at his tag and saw that his name was Daniel. That was the first time I met your father.

"After the service, I darted out toward the exits. Everyone was congregating in the aisles and the outer decks, and after he finished praying, Daniel made a mad dash to find me. I still remember how he started the conversation:

"Hi ma'am, how are you?"

"I'm well, thank you. Yourself?"

Daniel gushed, "Oh, I'm great. I'm fantastic, thank you! By the way I'm..."

I had already seen his nametag, so I finished his sentence. "...Daniel!"

His eyes were wide open, and I could see him notice my lips. I guess he was a bit caught off guard or tongue-tied because he said his name anyway.

"Yes, I'm Daniel, Daniel Durocher, and you are Jackie. I, I, I've noticed your nametag also. Incredibly pleased to meet you, Jackie."

"Me too!"

Daniel made some small talk about the service, then he said, "I think the world would be a better place if we had the courage to live by the principles the pastor was talking about."

"You mean abstinence?"

Daniel emphasized, "I meant all of it; the courtship instead of dating, getting to know the person before you get involved, asking all kinds of questions, and making sure they give answers; the person has to fear God, you know, and yes, abstinence too."

I wanted to take him down off his high horse a little bit, so I said, "But you know well that you men are the ones who start the trouble."

Daniel seemed confused and asked, "What do you mean?"

So, I took the gloves off. "Let's be serious, you guys are the ones who always do whatever it takes to get us in bed and then make us suffer afterward."

Daniel seemed troubled, but he responded with confidence. "Miss Jackie, there are decent guys out there who are genuine, thoughtful, and understanding. Like the pastor said, most women have the power to either give it away or to hold on to it, no matter how much pressure we men can give. And..."

I stopped him in the middle of his little speech and asked him, "And you believe that?"

With a smile of confidence, he said, "Yes, I do. Yes, I do believe most of you have the power to say no, Miss Jackie." He continued, "I agree with you that a lot of men will do whatever it takes to get you into their bed just to satisfy their lust. That's why you ladies, most of the time, have the last word. You have the ultimate decision."

"Wow! Ultimate decision," I replied, "that's a big word."

"I know!" Daniel said. "I meant to have a little plan like:

-Stay in-group

-Stay away from one on one dating

-Avoid alcohol (you are out on a date and he is coercing you to have more drinks just to cloud your sense of judgment). Well. You get the idea!

"Because, trust me, a lot of men will enjoy the moment if you let them."

"It was very interesting, Ananie. And somehow, maybe through my eyes, he found out that I was kind of enjoying the conversation. To tell you the truth, honey, I never had that kind of intense dialogue with a man before. It was always about other things like clubs, parties, gossip, and things like that.

"I liked the conversation very much, and the fact that he seemed willing to tell me the truth about some men who were only interested in getting between your legs. He asked me if I had time to sit down and talk some more. I looked at my watch and said, 'Okay, I have some time.' So, we went to a restaurant not too far.

"He offered me something to drink, but I rejected the favor. He insisted, so I decided to buy my own. After my past experiences, I had decided to be more cautious and prudent, even though he was supposedly a Christian."

"Am I boring you, baby?" Jackie asked her daughter since it was getting late.

Ananie exclaimed, "What? Are you kidding me, Mother? Do you have any idea how long I've been waiting for this moment to hear about you and Dad's romantic relationship?"

Jackie smiled and asked, "Okay, where were we again?"

Ananie was excited. "You refused to let him buy you a drink because of your past experiences with other men."

"Right, okay," Jackie said, and then she continued with her story:

Our first date was different, magical, and beautiful. We both ordered virgin margaritas, and then Daniel said, "You have an intriguing smile, a very beautiful lady, Miss Jackie! It felt like my heart skipped a beat for a second the moment I set eyes on you." He caught me off guard. I thanked him politely, and then he went right back into his speech about women having the power to say no.

He said something like, "The pastor was absolutely right because I have noticed that dressing modestly isn't a priority for many young women in the west, especially the United States. They expose way too much. Of course, this will get them a lot of attention, but often, it's the wrong attention. They're usually attracting the wrong men when they do that. Not only that, like Pastor Dennis said, even if they somehow meet up with a decent gentleman, they are exciting the wrong things in that man. They're, whether intentionally or unintentionally, appealing to the man's flesh. The Bible calls this lust."

Then he pointed to some young women at the bar and used them as his example. He said, "You see how they are dressed? They are showing things that only their future husbands should be allowed to see. If those women are here for the conference, it's even more tragic. They should know better.

"So, now you are judging them?" I said.

"Not at all, Jackie! Not at all!" replied Daniel. "But if we are Christians, every part of our life should be based on the truth of the Bible."

Then he wrapped up his speech by saying, "They are igniting lust in men by the way they dress. Jesus said that if a man looks at a woman with lust in his heart, it's the same as committing adultery. The Bible also says that we should not do anything that would cause our brothers to stumble. It's hard to argue that these women aren't guilty of setting up a stumbling block for their brothers."

He then explained that men are much more visual than women. He said it was a real struggle for young men to keep their thoughts pure, and women should dress modest as a courtesy to their brothers.

Then, to drive his point home further, he pointed out a few men in the room who were looking at three young women. He was right. These women were wearing dresses so tight you could see the imprint of their underwear.

It didn't stop there. The young women got up and walked by a table where some young men were sitting, and most of the young men reacted the same way, by ogling the women and shouting. Daniel seemed to feel bad for everyone involved.

He said, "Those young women are putting themselves and others in a bad situation. The sad thing is, many teenage girls are allowed to dress immodestly because their parents try to be their best friends. It's so easy for parents to rationalize this by telling themselves, 'She's a good kid. She doesn't drink or smoke. She's using her own money for the clothes. I guess it's okay. You can't fight every battle. You have to let them grow up.'

"But they are wrong. Everyone wants to have a good relationship with their children, but compromising our morals or failing to teach and train them properly isn't the way to get there."

With that, your father seemed done with his speech. By that time, I agreed with him.

Ananie spoke up. "Now I understand why you carefully chose my dresses."

Jackie shook her head and said, "That's right, baby."

"Anyway, I got it a long time ago. You don't have to worry about me in this area, Mom."

"I know that, honey," Jackie said. "So, back to that night."

Your dad turned his attention back toward me and said that I was sending a different message than those ladies. I said, "I beg your pardon?"

He explained his belief that we all intentionally or unintentionally send a message in the way we present ourselves. He said something like, "When a young lady is dressed conservatively, not revealing her body or being provocative, she is (unknowingly) sending a message that she is not interested in men who are looking for those things. She may be sending a message that she is a child of God and wants to honor Him by the way she dresses. The result is that the wrong kind of men can't even see her."

I asked him to explain, and he went on.

"There are some men that have sexual conquest as their primary interest. It's their main goal when interacting with young women. They are normally also the type of men who don't care if young women get hurt, or even if they get pregnant. The worst part is, they will often talk terribly about the young women they sleep with when they are around their friends. They will dishonor those young women, ruin their reputation, and speak about them like objects of pleasure. It's very sad."

I think Daniel could tell I was feeling a little upset, because then he said, "But the right kind of man, the godly man will never do those things. And he will still notice you even when you dress in a conservative way."

Your father then began speaking directly about me. He said, "When I look at you, I see a person who respects herself and others. You also display self-control and discipline." Then he said that he had noticed me ever since the first day of the conference. He called me a fabulous-looking queen and said he was interested in getting to know me.

I was a little shocked, and it made me a bit uncomfortable. Part of me wanted to stay, but I got up and told him I had to go.

Then, he was so bold, your father. Then he said, "I will respect you and never touch you until we get married."

This actually made me feel warmth in my heart, but I wasn't ready to open up to him like that. I had just met him. So, I said, "It was nice meeting you, Daniel." We exchanged phone numbers. My friend Johanna walked up, so I excused myself to go walk around with her.

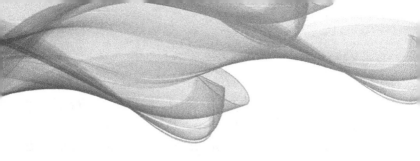

Chapter 4

The Revelation

*J*ackie and Ananie made some hot cocoa and continued their conversation. Ananie was eager to learn everything she could about her mom and dad's history together.

"So that was how we met," Jackie explained. "After that, we spent two years in courtship. He respected and loved me. He never pushed me or pressured me in any way. From time to time, we would find ourselves alone, in a moment of weakness, and we would quickly reverse course. Basically, we would turn and run from the temptation. If we kissed and felt ourselves getting excited in that way, we would say goodnight and leave each other. He definitely kept his promise to never touch me sexually until we got married.

"I remember the night before he proposed to me," Jackie explained before recounting the story to Ananie:

Gently and tenderly, your father said, "I feel I've been an open book with you, telling you about things in my past, my feelings, my views. But I feel you have never really opened up with me in that same way. I really hate surprises. Is there anything I should know about your past? I think it's best to talk about it now. We all make mistakes, right? Is there anything I should know?"

I panicked. I was afraid to tell him the truth because I thought I might lose him. I was completely head over heels in love with him by this time. All I wanted was to be with him and love him for the rest of my life. I wanted to grow old with him and live out our dreams together. Although I believe that God had used your dad to work in my life and give me a new perspective about what was good and healthy and right in dating and sex. But I was still ashamed of my past, so I lied.

With tears in her eyes, Jackie recounted how she had lied to Daniel. There was so much pain in her voice—so much anger and unforgiveness toward herself. Ananie asked her to stop, and then tried to change the subject. But Jackie wanted to continue:

I knew I couldn't tell your dad that I was a virgin, so I told him that I had only been with one man sexually. I told him it had not been very serious and that I had stayed single ever since then. I thought that if I could hide my past, bury it somehow, that I could start a new life with him.

Your dad and I had so much fun together. We fell in love with each other and could not resist one another.

The feelings were so strong every time we were together. I felt that I had a good life in front of me if I could just keep this secret from everyone, especially him.

Of course, it turned out to be a mistake. I realize now that if I had just told your father the truth, he would have loved me anyway and forgiven me. But instead, we started out based on lies. And lies always catch up with us in the end.

Two years after we married, we decided to take a small vacation. I was already seven months pregnant with you, and we knew things were going to be very different after that. We wanted to go have a little fun by taking a road trip to Washington DC.

We stopped at a restaurant for dinner. I remember your dad ordered fish. He loves fish. We were having a great time. Your father was very happy and excited to see you in a couple of months. I was excited too. It was a very happy time, but it didn't stay that way.

I had ordered some food to go, and he got up to go check on the order. At about that time, three of my old friends noticed me in the restaurant and came to my table; Eric, Tim, and McCoy. My heart stopped. I looked over at your father, who was now talking on the phone over by the bar.

He looked up at me and his face seemed to ask if everything was okay. I smiled at him and he went on talking. My old friends made some small talk. They seemed shocked that I was married and pregnant, but they congratulated me before excusing themselves.

When I looked up, Daniel was not there. I assumed he went to the restroom, so I waited patiently for a few minutes. But he didn't return. I waited and waited for fifteen minutes. I called his cell phone, and he picked it up. His response was so dry. Something had changed. I wasn't sure what, but the Daniel I knew was gone.

All he said was, "I will be right there." And then he hung up. He had never gotten off the phone before without telling me "diagridem" or "I love you."

He finally came back. He said he was in the restroom that whole time and that he wasn't feeling well. I knew something more was going on, but I didn't want to push anything. I was afraid to know the truth, so I just left it alone.

On our way back to Atlanta, he stayed quiet. We barely talked. I didn't feel my Daniel anymore. I have to tell you, Ananie, a lot of things were going through my mind, but I decided not to bring up any of it. I guess I was too afraid. Maybe I was hoping this would just pass, or it would turn out to be nothing.

After our trip, I felt that he was different. He tried to act normal, but I felt like he was only doing that out of a sense of duty to you. He felt strongly about breastfeeding for the health of the baby, and he knew I would need a lot of extra support while doing that. For the next two years, we lived together, but our relationship was always strained. Distant. Cold.

Finally, one day he decided to talk to me about what had happened. But when he did, I could tell that his mind was already made up. He had decided to end our marriage. We yelled at each other. He was deeply angry with me.

We agreed for him to be in your life, to be a father that could come by and see you anytime. I decided that I had made too many mistakes already in the area of dating, courtship, and marriage. I decided to remain alone and devoted myself to God and raising you.

Jackie thought that she had given Ananie a satisfactory explanation of her history with Daniel, but Ananie wasn't satisfied at all. "Mother!" she exclaimed. "I've been waiting all this time, and you're not going to tell me the whole story? What did Dad decide to talk to you about? What happened in that restaurant?"

An uncomfortable silence filled the room. Jackie didn't want to talk to her daughter about the details of her past mistakes, but she decided that it would be best for Ananie if she did. After all, parents are supposed to help their children make better decisions. Parents are supposed to impart wisdom and help their children with the lessons they wish someone had taught them. She decided to tell it all.

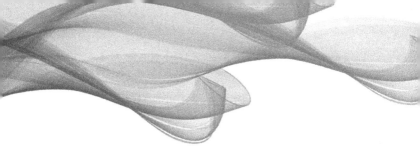

Chapter 5

The Secret Is Out

*Y*ou see, Ananie, when I was in high school, I wasn't doing very well. I wasn't paying good attention in class. My parents had divorced, and your grandmother was working two jobs to take care of us. There were four of us kids still in the house with her, growing up and getting into all kinds of things. She did the best she could, but she barely had time for any of us.

We all had our own key to the house and could come and go whenever we wanted. I used to spend most of my time just hanging out with friends, going places I probably shouldn't have gone. I ended up getting into the party scene. First, it was alcohol and sex, and later on, I even tried drugs.

After that, I had many sexual partners, including Tim and McCoy, two out of the three men at the restaurant. They were all athletes. Back then, it was like a badge of honor for me to sleep with them.

Everyone looked up to them. They were popular, almost like stars at our high school, and I was drawn to that. McCoy gave me drugs. Ananie, sex and drugs can feel very good in that moment. The Bible says in Hebrews 11:25 that sin brings pleasure for a season, and it is very true.

But they say in church, "Sin will take you further than you wanted to go, keep you longer than you wanted to stay, and cost you more than you wanted to pay." That is also very true, my sweet daughter.

Later, I started messing around with Tim. They were all friends, and I guess they just sort of passed around different girls like property. All I know is that McCoy stopped calling me about the same time Tim started approaching me. So, I thought, why not?

Later on, I got pregnant by him. I wanted to have the baby. I thought, even though we were young, we could graduate, get married, and raise the child together. But he pressured me to have an abortion.

Once I agreed and went through with it, he dumped me. He stopped coming around or calling me. I decided to ask him one day at school why he wasn't coming around. He brought me aside and told me that he wasn't ready to get married or have children. Then he said something that really hurt. He said, "If I ever do decide to get married and have kids, it won't be with a girl like you."

I felt humiliated. I was deeply ashamed of myself. How could I be so stupid? Yes, I knew that the original plan for these guys was just being young and having fun, but life happened. Something serious had happened, and no one cared. I didn't realize until that moment what *little these guys thought of me. I was like a disposable play toy to them.*

It was an eye opener. I could see that these "friends" had no concern for my feelings. None of the people I was hanging around cared about what I was going through. None of them cared about what I was feeling. They just wanted to drink more, do more drugs, go to more parties, and have more sex. Anything that might put a damper on their good time was unwelcome.

After that, I basically decided to get away from that life. I told my mom everything, and she sent me to live with my grandmother in Atlanta. My grandmother took me to church and taught me a lot about life. In regard to guys, I decided to stay away from them for the most part, at least until I knew I had met the right guy.

At that point, Ananie felt terrible for her mom. They cried together and shared some hugs. Ananie wanted to fix everything, but she couldn't. At the same time, Jackie wanted to make sure Ananie fully understood the destruction and pain she had experienced, so she launched into a speech to help drive the point home as honestly and powerfully as she could:

Ananie, I want you to know this, not because I want you to feel worse for me than you already do. But I want you to understand how much I have suffered for my past mistakes. I still suffer for them. My marriage was taken from me because of mistakes I made in high school.

I wish I could go back and fix these things. I wish I could go back and do everything over. I would give almost anything, but actions always have consequences.

If you were to go out and have sex right now, you could get pregnant. There's no way to undo that. People think they can undo it through abortion, but that baby still exists. That life was still created, and all abortion does is take that life unlawfully, according to God's law.

Yes, Jesus offers us forgiveness and redemption. But we often still bear our scars and suffer earthly consequences for the things we do. We have to recognize that there can be terrible consequences for sin. But it only helps so much to recognize that bad things can happen and then try to avoid those bad things.

Really, the best way to avoid doing wrong things is to immerse yourself in doing all of the right things. That's why education and church life are so crucial for young people. If a young person is spending all of their time and energy getting ahead, learning, developing, growing, and building character, they don't have time and energy left over to get into all kinds of wrong and destructive things—things like alcohol, sex, and drugs.

Besides that, you are building a better future for yourself. Education and hard work can open all kinds of doors for you and allow you to walk through them with dignity and self-respect. Not only that, you'll have the respect of others.

On the other hand, fifteen minutes of sex can drastically change your life. It can lead you to a lifetime of painful regret. You basically have to get to a place where you take a moment, talk to the Lord, and make a decision about who you want to be and the kind of life you want to lead.

If you choose abstinence, that's the best way to ensure a stable, healthy life ahead of you. One day, you will meet a nice young man. You'll fall in love and get married. Then, you can have sex any time you want for the rest of your life. It's hard to wait through high school, but it can be done.

Even if you don't get pregnant, sexual sin carries a consequence that no other sin carries. It can hurt you physically, mentally, emotionally, and spiritually. There is a principle that often gets repeated in church, "Sleep with someone and you sleep with everyone they've slept with."

That's not literally true, but it's true in some ways. For example, you have the same risk of incurable disease, like AIDS or hepatitis that you would have if you slept with everyone they slept with. But even if that doesn't happen, there is a sense in which you are uniting spiritually with someone during sex. You can unite with your husband one day, and the union will have God's protection and blessing.

But if you unite with people who are not your husband, the union will not have God's protection and blessing. 1 Corinthians 6:15-16 says, "Do you not know that your bodies are members of Christ? Shall I then take the members of Christ and make them members of a prostitute? Never! Or do you not know that he who is joined to a prostitute becomes one body with her? For, as it is written, 'The two will become one flesh.'"

Sexual union is a serious thing. When people engage in various sins, they open doors in the spiritual realm. They give the devil license to occupy that territory in their lives. In the case of sexual sin, they are giving the devil license to their bodies.

The devil only comes to steal, kill, and destroy. That is what God says in 1 Corinthians 6:18, "Flee from sexual immorality. Every other sin a person commits is outside the body, but the sexually immoral person sins against his own body."

With sexual sin, we are inviting destruction into our bodies. Sex is a great thing and meant to be enjoyed in a union between husband and wife. When that is the case, God blesses it, and it's a very, very good thing. But when it happens outside of that blessing and protection, it is sin, and sin always brings destruction of some kind.

In my case, my sexual past haunted me and destroyed my marriage.

The bottom line, Ananie, is that if a man loves you and he is a good Christian man, he will wait. If he refuses, then he's not the one.

Ananie thanked her mom for sharing her heartfelt advice. She said, "Mom, you know I agree with all of this already."

Jackie responded, "I know, honey, but sometimes our commitment, our convictions, and our principles get tested. I want to make sure I've done everything in my power to help you make the right decisions."

"You have, Mom. You have done that, and I'm grateful."

Ananie did not want to press her mother to share any more painful details of what happened back then. They hugged each other tightly and retired for the night.

Chapter 6

The Sleepover

*J*ohanna was one of Jackie's longtime friends from elementary school, and throughout high school, they partied together until Jackie decided to turn her life around. Although they barely hang out anymore as adults, they always kept the lines of communication open. Johanna recently received an unexpected promotion and needed to spend the next few days out of town for job training, so she called Jackie out of the blue and asked her if she would let her daughter Stacey stay at her house over the weekend. Although Jackie was aware that her daughter and Stacey were not good buddies in the past, she accepted the challenge.

Ananie and Stacey had known each other through school, but they were not friends. Stacey was, in fact, very mean to Ananie by calling her names, such as "Old fashioned," "Virgin Mary," Daddy's little girl," just to name a few.

Stacey arrived, and Jackie explained their house rules. Ananie came downstairs and greeted Stacey warmly, even giving her a hug and complimenting her hair. Stacey was surprised but pleased by her kindness. They talked for a while, played some card games, and ate some pizza. It was a pleasant evening.

Shortly after cleaning the dining room, Ananie and Stacey went into the den to hang out and talk away from Jackie.

"I have to tell you, at first, I wasn't sure about spending three days here. I felt really uncomfortable when my mom told me I was coming," Stacey explained honestly.

"Why?" asked Ananie.

"Because of the way my friends and I treated you."

"Oh, that," replied Ananie. "Yes, you guys were pretty hard on me," Ananie admitted.

Stacey continued, "You just always dressed so conservatively and never seemed to have any fun. You were never at parties. I'm sorry we gave you such a hard time. Thank you for being so nice to me since I got here."

"You're welcome, Stacey. School was hard for me at times, but my parents trained me to handle the rejection and difficulties," Ananie explained.

"You did always seem to just smile and keep working away from our intimidation. You may have called it bullies also," Stacey said before asking an important question. "How did your parents train you?"

"Well, they taught me how to choose my friends. They said that a friend is someone who shares my values and has a positive impact on me. They said I should look for people who have great qualities that are worthy of imitation because friends will always rub off on us and influence us. Lastly, they said that a friend should always be loyal, as the Bible says in Proverbs 17:17, 'A friend loves at all times.'

Stacey responded, half-joking, "Now I see why you stayed away from us," as they decided to go up to Ananie's room. The first thing Stacey noticed was how well organized everything was. She wondered aloud how Ananie could keep everything so neat and tidy.

Ananie explained, "Well, I'm used to it at this point. Since I was little, my mom and dad always taught me to work hard, stay organized, and be resourceful. They even taught me how to fix things around the house, cook meals…"

"Wait a minute! You know how to cook?" Stacey interjected, surprisingly.

"Yes. At first, I used to mess everything up in the kitchen pretty badly. But it just takes some practice and good instruction. I remember when I was a little girl, my dad used to make everything fun. He even tried to make study time seem fun. I always had to finish my homework before I could watch TV. My parents even made me go to bed early every night except on the weekends.

"It all seemed hard when I was going through it, but now I look back and I'm grateful because I've developed good habits that will go with me into adulthood. On the other hand, most people our age don't even know how to do basic stuff to take care of themselves.

"But Mom always sat me down and walked me through paying bills. We paid the mortgage and car insurance the first of every month, and she paid most other bills on the fifteenth of every month. She even had me open a bank account and taught me to save. I have over twenty-five hundred dollars in there right now."

"You're kidding," Stacey said.

"No, I'm serious. Like I said, I wasn't always happy about the way they were teaching me and training me as I grew up. But in the last eight years, I've started to understand the benefits of it and to appreciate it. I feel very blessed to have such good parents," Ananie explained.

"You're going to think this is really crazy, but my dad even has a dress code."

"What?" asked Stacey, surprised. "How do your parents even find time to do all of this stuff?"

"They make time. My dad has even taken me on dates. He would explain to me from Proverbs 20:29 that being self-governed is vital for godly young men to control lust. They must have a clear vision, and direction for the path they choose. They need to know how to take responsibility for their actions. 'The glory of young men is their strength.'"

"Okay, that's weird," Stacey blurted out.

"No, it sounds weird, but it isn't. He further talked about actions and feelings, clear and honest communication to compromise, when needed, without compromising itself. In general, self-controlled to make godly decisions. He would just take me out to explain and show me how a real gentleman should act; that way, I would know what kind of man to look for," Ananie explained.

"And how does a real gentleman act?" Stacey asked.

"Well, he would always open the car door for me. When we would get somewhere, he would get out first and go around and open the door for me again. Then when we got to the restaurant, he would stand behind my chair and pull it out for me to sit down. He continued. The normal way is to live and act by principles, not by emotions. A man with honor is a man who is admired, trusted, and respected. The people around him judge him as a good person.

"When you think of acts of service, it can be massive. A young man cannot just say a kind word or give a quick kiss to you and think it is good enough. Showing love through acts of service takes effort, and most of all, vigilance.

"Even if he is a guy who is the old-fashioned sort who likes to treat his lady when out on a date, he must cover the bills and also help with chores after marriage. This is trickier when you are only dating, so be sensitive to acts of service that might cross your way.

"Another key point for a real gentleman is quality time. Taking time out of our day for the people we love is a way of expressing what we feel. Quality time is the love language that centers on togetherness. It is all about expressing love and affection with your undivided attention.

"It was simple and basic things like that, but he explained so much to me. He told me about young men and how they should treat a lady that gave me a lot of confidence.

"I know what to look for, and I'm not going to run to some guy who doesn't treat me well. I think it has helped me prepare well for dating and courtship. I don't feel any desperation or any need to get attention from guys. I don't need to attract many guys. I'm only interested in finding the one right guy someday."

"What else did your parents teach you?" Stacey was becoming interested at this point.

"Well, they taught me table manners and how to effectively use the different utensils. My dad talked about how to present myself in social situations, how it's easier to carry a positive mindset than a negative one. He taught me to treat others with respect, to be kind to everyone, but to take care of myself as well."

"Oh my gosh, this is so weird, but in a good way. What else did he teach you?" Stacy asked.

"Let's see...to always take responsibility for my actions. Admit when I'm wrong. Apologize, but don't make excuses. Always tell the truth, even when I've messed up. He does encourage me to have fun too."

"Fun, how? None of that sounds like fun," Stacey interjected.

"Well, I play tennis and basketball. Those are a lot of fun. I like to watch movies with my parents or friends, play card games and board games, that kind of stuff."

"Okay, yeah. I guess that's fine, but what about getting out of the house?"

"Well, we sometimes go out to the movies and the museum. We visit the MLK center and learn more about our history. My dad says we should never stop learning. He says success in life comes from focus, dedication, and hard work."

"Forgive me for what I'm about to ask you," said Stacey.

"No problem," replied Ananie.

"I've been listening to you for a while now, but everything you've told me is precisely what your parents want or demand from you. What about your own thoughts, your own desires, without your parents' approval? Do they allow you to freely express your...I don't know...yourself? Have your own opinion?"

"Absolutely, Stacey," Ananie replied, "otherwise, I would not be so proud of talking to you about my parents' interaction with me.

"I felt compelled to let my folks take the credits instead of bragging about myself. As I became older, my parents lectured me less. Instead, we communicate more often.

"Stacey, for the past eight years and counting, I have the privilege to express my thoughts, my concerns, and be able to tell my parents what was bothering me during the "Express Yourself" meeting.

"What's that?" Stacey asked.

"Almost every weekend during dinner time, I got a chance to freely express myself to my mom and dad about what I liked or disliked during the past week. We would also find a solution to make it right together." "Interesting!" said Stacey.

"Also, I have the privilege to present my ideas, my own personal view to my family, and that draws me closer to them. By the way, you will have an opportunity to be part of our "Express Yourself" meeting this weekend. It will be fun," said Ananie.

"I cannot wait!" Stacey shouted.

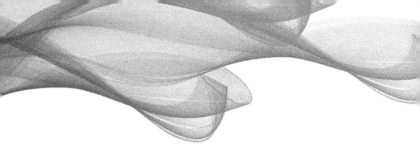

Chapter 7

The Father's Advice on Dating

*A*nanie continued telling Stacey about the things her father taught her. She explained that instead of dating, he used the terms "courting" and "courtship." She also explained that her parents introduced various topics to her over time.

"The way they talked to me when I was ten years old is different than the way they talked to me when I was fifteen. I think they tried to make sure they were discussing appropriate topics at appropriate times," Ananie explained.

"You mean like boyfriends and sex?" Stacey inquired.

"Yes...I mean, Dad always said us young people were going to get information about those things from somewhere, and it should be from our parents first and foremost."

"So, what did he say about sex?"

"He said that sex was one of the many beautiful things that God created for humankind."

"He actually said that?" Stacey asked, confused. "I thought parents only acted like sex was bad and wrong if they talked about it at all."

"I was surprised, too, when he first brought it up. It felt kind of weird and uncomfortable until we got talked. Then it started to feel like something we should be talking about."

"So, your dad lets you have sex?"

"No! Not at all!" Ananie exclaimed. "He just explained to me the importance of going about it all the right way, that God intended sex only for marriage, and that God doesn't bless sex outside of marriage. Sex outside of marriage is actually under the curse of sin, and that's why it has so many destructive consequences.

"He also said that females have a lot more power and control in this area than they realize. Many females treat their sexuality as a 'little thing' when, in fact, it is anything but little. It is very powerful and very valuable. It should never be given away to a man who is not your husband.

"He also warned me that many young men will say and do just about anything to get what isn't rightfully theirs."

"You mean sex? Yeah, they certainly will do that," Stacey agreed. "So, Ananie, have you ever had sex?"

"No, I'm waiting for marriage. I guess all of Dad's talks worked because I don't feel any need to go out and give away what rightfully belongs to my future husband. That being said, I am looking forward to getting married as soon as I meet the right young man!"

"You want to get married now while you're young?" Stacey asked.

"Yes, of course. Why wouldn't I?" Ananie shot back.

"Well, to be young, have fun, not be tied down. I don't know, live a little."

"I think a godly marriage is going to be way fun. I can't think of anything more fun than being together with a good Christian man and enjoying each other's company. I think of going on romantic dates, taking trips together, and serving God together. And having lots of sex! It's going to be amazing!"

They both laughed.

"I guess you're right. That does sound more fun than having guys use you and then treat you like dirt later on. Trust me, that's not fun at all," said Stacey.

"I'm sorry that happened to you, Stacey. The good news is, you can start right now turning things around. Jesus loves you. He wants you to come to Him with all of your hurts and your mistakes. He wants to forgive you and heal you. He will do it!" Ananie encouraged her.

"So how do I do that? How do you come to Jesus?" Stacey asked.

"Well, you just pray. You say something like this:

Lord, I have made a lot of mistakes in my life. I've committed a lot of sins. I need you to save me, heal me, and make me clean. I come to you, Jesus, and I give my life to you.

"Once you do that, He will come in and immediately start changing you. You'll never be the same," Ananie explained.

"Can I do it right now?" Stacey asked, with tears in her eyes.

"Yes! Let's do it right now!"

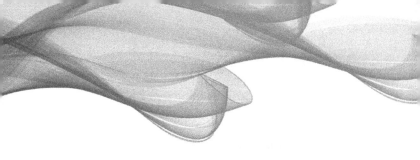

Chapter 8

Stacey's New Beginning

*A*fter praying and giving her life to Jesus, Stacey almost immediately began to realize that there were things in her life she needed to stop doing that would hurt her, that she would probably regret for the rest of her life.

She began to tell Ananie about some of those things. Stacey explained how she would sneak out at night after her mother went to bed. She would go to parties, drink alcohol, smoke pot, and have sex. She had even been involved in some particularly embarrassing sexual episodes while under the influence of alcohol and drugs, not remembering who she had sexual contact with at certain parties.

She began to weep over her bad choices.

Ananie assured her that it was okay. She was forgiven, washed clean by the blood of Jesus. She now would go through a process called sanctification, where Jesus would help free her of all the temptations she's dealt with, as well as being healed of the destructive behaviors.

On Sunday evening, Johanna stopped by to pick up Stacey. Johanna thanked Jackie for her hospitality. Before they left, Stacey told Ananie and Jackie how grateful she was for the time they had together.

"I have learned so much in my short time here. My life has been changed. Thank you very much," Stacey said.

Ananie responded, "It was my pleasure. I also want to leave you with this message that I believe the Lord is putting on my heart for you. This is a new beginning for you, Stacey. The Lord wants you to leave the past behind and move forward with Him."

Stacey thanked Ananie and Jackie again and was on her way. While she walked out to the car, she felt about a million pounds lighter-almost as if she could fly away.

The thought of a new beginning with God filled her soul with joy!

Unfortunately, her mother didn't meet her joy with much enthusiasm.

"What was that all about?" Johanna said, after slamming her car door.

"What?" Stacey asked.

Johanna said sternly, "That emotional scene about your life being changed. What was that?"

"Well, this weekend was really good for me. I learned some things, things I wish I had learned a long time ago."

Her mother stopped her with an ugly attitude. "Wait! Wait! Wait! You've learned from whom? Jackie? Jackie? Child, please! You are talking about Jackie? Are you serious or what? Stacey you don't know that woman the way we knew her," Johanna continued with enjoyment. "That slut? Why do you think her husband left her in the first place? Because he found out that she was a slut. Well! All of a sudden, she becomes what? A counselor now? The fact remains, honey! Now that promiscuous woman might calm herself down because she is so consumed with guilt, pains, all the failures, all that crap. So, don't you sit down here and portray Jackie like some angel because she isn't!" Johanna barked.

"You are missing the point," Stacey said mournfully. "It's not about Jackie anymore, Mother! It's all about her daughter now. Can't you see that? She's preparing her for a better life, a better tomorrow; that's what matters to me. Whatever happened in Mrs. Jackie's past, she's trying her best to prevent her daughter from doing the same thing, and that's a good thing." Stacey continued with conviction, her eyes wide open, "That's admirable and beautiful!

"You know what, Mother? I thank God for the past three days." Stacey smiled a bit and continued, "I actually got to experience what it's like to have good and kind communication with someone else, Mother. The funny thing was that my friends and l used to make fun of Ananie. We used to call her a nun, Daddy's daughter, and old-fashioned.

"Do you know why, Mother? Because she was different and refused to do things that l thought were all right or cool at that time. Now I understand why she refused to get involved in our stupidity. She has parents who care about her and her future, but that is not true for me."

Stacey's mother hit the brakes hard and pulled over to the side of the road. She then slapped Stacey twice and yelled, "How dare you!"

"What the heck gives you the right to say something like that?" With anger in her face, she continued, "I'm busting my butt with two jobs to take care of you, keeping a roof over your crazy head, and now that is how you thank me, right?" Johanna demanded.

Stacey screamed louder, "But I need a mother too!"

"That's right! I need someone who cares about me! Me! Yes, me! Show me that I'm important, chat with me, prepare me for tomorrow, for the challenges that I'm going to face. You had your experiences in life, and you've learned lessons. Why didn't you tell me those things? Yes, sometimes I may not act like I want to hear it, but you say them anyway because that is what parents do, show their children that they always care about them.

"It's not just about providing food, clothes, and a place to stay. Yes, I appreciate that, but we also need love, attention, and communication! That's what I need from you as well!"

For a moment, there was complete silence inside the car. While Stacey wiped her tears with her t-shirt, Johanna faced straight forward, unflinching. Stacey somehow got her mother's attention and then continued with a softer tone and more self-control.

"The last time you actually spoke to me for more than a few minutes was when I told you I saw blood in my underwear. I was 12 years old, Mother, 12 years old, and do you remember your response? Your response was 'Now you can get pregnant, so don't go out there messing around with those men.' That was it. Oh! Oh! I forgot because you were getting late for your second job.

"At least I was expecting you to say, 'honey, I'm late for work, I promise you we'll talk about it later,' or whatever. But I barely see you during the week because I have my own key to get home whenever I want, right? And on Sunday, that's when you watch all the recorded soap operas from last week. We never have mother-daughter time together. Never. Never!" Stacey struggled for a moment again before composing herself.

"But during the last three days, I found out that I'm a valuable and beautiful young woman. They told me I could achieve anything I wanted in life. They told me I shouldn't attract the wrong men by the way I dress, and a conservative appearance would be more appropriate and safe.

"And when I asked them what was appropriate and safe, they told me anywhere between my private parts and knees should be kept covered. I've learned to stay away from clubs and the wrong kind of parties. I've learned that I should talk to my mother to choose which friends' parties I should attend. I learned that even at good parties, I should keep my drink in my hands all the time. In case I did forget it at the table, I should not drink it anymore because there are some bad people out there who can make me do things against my will by adding stuff to my drink.

"By the way, Miss Jackie also told me to stay away from alcohol because it can be very dangerous for a young lady. I was told, also, to take my time when it comes to relationships, especially at my age. Most of the men will tell me that I'm beautiful or will do any-thing to have sex with me, and once they get what they want, they are the ones who are going to trash me with their friends, and friends after friends will know about it, and in no time I can forget about my good reputation nor my family too.

"But she said when I wait for sex, whatever the pressure, not to give up until the right time. People are going to call me a bunch of names like 'Daddy's little girl,' or they will say, 'Go ahead, save it for Jesus,' and laugh at me, provoking me to want to give it away! But I will not!

"Miss Jackie said I will see how much respect I earn in the long run, especially from the ones who used to trash me. Miss Jackie told me that I will have all the time in the world to enjoy sex because every time I have sex with a different person, I give a part of my soul away. She told me that keeping myself pure till my wedding night does not guarantee a happy life ever after either, but she told me right now, education is the best key that can get me anywhere at any door I want to open.

"She said to take full advantage while I'm still young because I can learn quicker and faster than I am able later on. She told me to read more often, learn to play an instrument, or get involved in sports—basically to keep myself busy and stay away from bad influences.

"Now I know why Ananie stayed away from my group. And the last thing she told me, she said on top of everything, God has to be first in my life, and once I put *Him* above all, He will lead me.

"She read something from Proverbs 31:30, 'Favor is deceitful, and beauty is vain: but a woman that feared the LORD, she shall be praised.'

"Not bad, Mother! Not bad at all for someone you call names! By the way, According to the Bible, Mrs. Jackie is a new person. In the New King James Version, 2 Corinthians 5:17 says, '*Therefore, if anyone is in Christ, he is a new creation; old things have passed away: behold, all things have become new.'*

"The old Jackie is gone, Paul writes. The new has come. That means all the old dreams and ideas and agenda and purposes have ceased to exist and Christ's ideas have replaced them.

"I'm just saying I believe God sent me to Mrs. Jackie's house so I can turn my life around because..." Stacey paused a few seconds as if she was replaying all of the major moments in her life. Then, she finally let out her conclusion, "Because I started in the wrong direction, I mean big time."

All of a sudden, Johanna's demeanor had changed. The angry mom who had been slapping, yelling, and cussing at her daughter to show that she was in charge just a little while ago was now gone. She went cold, not even a word, nada, zero.

It's as if Stacey hit her conscience with a big-time hammer. She stayed very quiet, looking down for a while. Her face displayed remorse, shame, and disappointment in herself. Tears came down, and she finally raised her head, but kept looking straight ahead. She wiped her face with her hands and said, "18 years ago, I was young, beautiful, and immature. Maybe I should say stupid. I thought I was completely in control and untouchable because of my beauty. I had a nice body. Men were attracted to me. I thought I was on top of the world. My parents gave me everything I wanted.

"I had a chance to become whatever I wanted, but I listened to myself and my friends who told me that my parents and theirs were old school. We decided that they just didn't want us to enjoy being young, that they wanted us to stay with their old-school mindset. At first, it made sense what my friends were saying because my mom and, especially, my grandma Regine, always had a message to preach to me.

"And I still can hear her voice whisper in my head, 'Daughter! Daughter! You know that you are a beautiful young lady, you need to be very careful...blah blah blah! Just like all the stuff Jackie was telling you. But, unfortunately, I've had to learn all of my lessons the hard way. I didn't listen.

"If I am not mistaken, it was a Friday, December 31, 1993. I went to a party with my friends. I was having a lot of fun, and the next thing I remember," she paused a bit like she was reliving a painful experience, before continuing, "I woke up naked in the bed of a cheap motel, and I couldn't even remember how I got there.

"There are no words to even describe how I felt at that moment. A lot of things went through my head. I even thought about suicide. Then I remembered my grandma used to say to never take that road, it doesn't matter how bad or low the situation. Suicide was a *no, no, no...never.*

I spent at least two hours inside the room crying so hard that the person next door came banging on my door. He asked me if I wanted him to call 911, and

I declined. I went downstairs to the front desk, and the person in charge told me that he didn't have any info regarding that room.

"His guess was that someone must have paid cash, and since He wasn't on duty, he couldn't tell me anything. I left the motel with the idea that I may never know who did that to me. I had lost my purse and I didn't have any money to take a cab, so I had to walk several miles to get home.

"Upon my arrival, my brothers and sisters were extremely mad at me. I had lied to my parents, saying that I spent the night at Fabienne's house. Although she covered for me, my father was still angry with me. He said that I should have called them. He hit me so hard, and then he used strong language to show me how furious he was.

"Honestly, Stacey, part of me was not even in the room when my parents were yelling at me. Almost everything in me was still trying to make sense of how in the world I got to that motel. Suddenly, my grandma came to mind when she used to tell me to keep my drink close to me and always be careful when I would go to a friend's party, and so on. But it was too late because 3 months later, I found out that I was pregnant.

"I wanted to have an abortion so badly because I was scared, but you were almost four months in my womb; not only was it too risky, but I was about to kill a human being. My grandma always said if there is life in the infant, it doesn't matter if he or she was four months or one month; if you have an abortion, that's murder. In human eyes, it might be fine, but in the eyes of God, it's a grave sin.

"I thought about all that and decided to run away because I knew I couldn't ever stand in front of my dad telling him that news. I wrote them a letter explaining my mistake, and that I did not dare stand before them all when I knew I was wrong. You see, I was afraid, especially of my dad. He was so sensitive about his reputation, his name in the community. I decided to take my responsibility on my own and stay away from them and their community.

"I went to my Aunt Marly. She wasn't happy about what happened to me, but she also refused to let me handle it by myself. Therefore, she allowed me to stay at her house as long as I wanted to. A few months after I had you, she advised me to return to school. I did, and since I had a thing for the medical field, I decided to study respiratory therapy. And I was glad I did it because three years later, after my auntie passed, I was able to care for you."

"Oh my God! Mother!" Stacey said, shocked. "I...I...I don't know what to say. I'm deeply sorry about that, Mother!"

"Well, there is nothing to be sorry about, honey, the problem was and is me. I was so ashamed of my past for what I've done. I thought if I kept myself busy with two jobs, or a nasty attitude, that would protect me from ever having to open up to anyone else—especially to you. I really thought hiding the truth from you about my past, your dad, and my parents would somehow make me feel better.

"Well! Today, once again, I find out that I was dead wrong. My God! You see, Stacey!" Johanna paused a little bit. Her right hand covered her mouth. She cried as though her soul was bleeding, like she'd been holding on to this pain and emotions for a very long time.

Stacey felt so bad. She spoke up, "Mother, can we stop, at least for tonight?"

Johanna declined her suggestion by waving her right hand and shaking her head. She finally got herself together and said, "I can't stop now. The madness and shame was inside of me for too long. I think it's time to finally let them go in the past where they belong.

"You never had a mother-daughter conversation simply because I wasn't fit to be your mother. Not only was I not prepared to handle that responsibility by myself, but at the same time, I was afraid you might ask me some personal questions that I was unwilling to answer. The day you asked about your puberty, I panicked. I didn't know how to answer you. But I can tell you, Stacey, that your mother right now—she is a new woman and ready to answer all of your questions.

"I'm grateful for the time you spent at Jackie's. Please forgive me, my daughter, for not being a real mother to you."

"Oh, come on, Mother," said Stacey. "Give me a hug. I love you so much, and of course, I forgive you. I'm so sorry for all things I have done to you and to God as well." Stacey looked up at the sky and said, "Thank you, God, for everything."

A few months later, Stacey got baptized. Then she began to invite her mother, Johanna, to go to church with her. At first, Johanna kept saying, "I'm just not a church person. My parents forced me to go to church and all they talked about was following all of these rules or God would be mad at me. As a result, I said I was never going to do that to you."

"But that's the thing, Mom. It's not about rules. It's about knowing God, the God who loves you, who created you, who was willing to die on a cross for you so that you could have abundant life. And the rules are just about keeping us safe and helping us do what's best for us. He just wants the best for us..."

"Well I am so happy for you, honey," said Johanna. "But I am just not into the Jesus stuff right now."

Consequently, Stacey and Johanna began to spend more quality time together. Stacey continued praying and reading her Bible. She began to change, and the change was noticeable. Stacey realized she couldn't force her mom to be interested in God or the Bible, so she decided to just love her mom and spend more time with her instead.

After a couple of months, Johanna began wanting to know more about what drove this change in Stacey. Thus, Johanna decided to try out Stacey's new church, and she loved it.

"Oh, my goodness, that church is so...different! I loved it," She said as they were leaving.

"I'm glad you liked it, Mom."

"It wasn't anything like the churches I went to growing up. This church is not like that. It's...so..." Johanna struggled for words.

"Life-giving?" Stacey offered a little help.

"Yes! Life-giving. Exactly! I feel energized. I feel...happy. I definitely don't feel like they're mad or judging me. I want to go back sometime for sure." Johanna explained.

A few more months passed, and Johanna was not doing well. The men in her life had disappointed her over and over through the years. Johanna had always been very beautiful. Her beauty had brought her a lot of things in life: favor, attention, and even financial success. But in the end, she had been left cold. Damaged. Heartbroken.

As she sat sobbing alone on the couch, she remembered that day she had gone to church with Stacey. She remembered the happiness, the joy she felt there. She had not felt like that in many years. Maybe she had never felt that way, actually.

Then she realized something. Over the last few months, her daughter seemed to have been that way all the time! Stacey seemed happy and joyful everyday! She thought to herself, *I've got to go back to that church.*

So the next worship service, she went with Stacey. But this worship service was different for Johanna. She didn't feel the same happiness. She had a feeling there was something serious going on inside her. She knew deep down that she had lived life her own way, had turned away from God early in life, and decided to live the way she wanted to live.

As the music played softly toward the end of the message, she felt a pull inside of her. *What is going on?* she wondered. *Why don't I feel happy?*

At that moment, the pastor said, "The reason some of you don't find joy and happiness in your life is that you're trying to live your life without God. You want to feel His joy. You want His life, light, and peace, but there's just one problem-you've shut God out of your life."

"It's time to let Him in," the pastor concluded.

At that moment, he gave an invitation to anyone who wanted to know God and surrender their life to Him.

With tears streaming down her face, Johanna raised her hand.

Everyone was supposed to have their heads bowed in reverence, but Stacey couldn't help but to sneak a peek. She knew the Lord had been working on her mom, and she had been praying for this moment for the last several months. No way was she going to miss it!

In that moment, Johanna prayed and gave her life to Jesus Christ. He entered her spirit and her heart as she prayed:

Lord, I have lived life my own way. I thought You just didn't want me to have any fun or enjoy life. But now I realize I was wrong. You only wanted what was best for my daughter and me. I'm so sorry, God. Please forgive me for all the things I've done wrong. I give my life to You, Jesus.

Like Stacey, Johanna was now a daughter of the King! She was adopted into God's family as His daughter-and a full heir of the eternal inheritance He has waiting for His children. She never again has to fear or worry about where she will spend eternity. She will be with God forever, and He will be with her in a place of beauty, love, and pleasures forevermore.

Then I saw "a new heaven and a new earth," for the first heaven and the first earth had passed away, and there was no longer any sea. I saw the Holy City, the new Jerusalem, coming down out of heaven from God, prepared as a bride beautifully dressed for her husband. And I heard a loud voice from the throne saying, "Look! God's dwelling place is now among the people, and he will dwell with them. They will be his people, and God himself will be with them and be their God. 'He will wipe

*every tear from their eyes. There will be no more death'
or mourning or crying or pain, for the old order of things
has passed away."*

*He who was seated on the throne said, "I am making
everything new!" Then he said, "Write this down, for
these words are trustworthy and true."*

*He said to me: "It is done. I am the Alpha and the
Omega, the Beginning and the End. To the thirsty I will
give water without cost from the spring of the water of
life. Those who are victorious will inherit all this, and I
will be their God and they will be my children. But the
cowardly, the unbelieving, the vile, the murderers, the
sexually immoral, those who practice magic arts, the
idolaters and all liars—they will be consigned to the
fiery lake of burning sulfur. This the second death"* Rev.
21:1-8 (NIV).

Johanna went into church that day as part of
the second group. She was part of the cowardly,
the unbelieving, and the sexually immoral. But she
walked out that day as part of the first group. She
was now included in God's people. Her eternal desti-
nation had been changed from one that is called "the
second death" to one that is called, "New Heaven,"
"New Earth," "The Holy City," "God's Dwelling Place."

You, dear reader, can make that same exchange
right now. You do not have to be in church to do
this. All you need to do is pray to Him and mean it
in your heart:

God, I give my life to You. I confess that I have gone my own way. I have sinned. I have done things that are wrong. I have done things that You say not to do, and I have hurt others and myself in the process. I want to give You my life now. I want to live Your way. I receive Jesus into my heart as Lord and Savior. I believe in Your Son, Jesus, with my heart, and with my mouth, I confess that He is my Lord, my Savior, my God. I know that my life will never be the same again, and I thank You for that, Lord. Thank You for loving me and saving me.

Chapter 9

A Breakthrough for Daniel

A short time after Ananie heard the story about her mom and dad's history, she had some questions for her dad. Therefore, she called and invited him on one of their dates.

During lunch, Daniel could tell that Ananie had something else on her mind. She didn't want to bring it up in the restaurant, so she was anxious to eat and be on their way.

After lunch, they went for a walk in the park. Ananie explained that Jackie had shared some of the story about their history and that she wanted to hear the rest from her dad.

"What is the reason you left Mom? Was it because of her history with the men you ran into at that restaurant?" Ananie inquired.

Daniel felt like he'd been hit with a hammer. He felt like his heart had stopped. His eyes began to water and turn red, and he began to speak slowly.

From day one, when I first met your mother, I put her on a pedestal. In my eyes, she was the most wonderful, most pure, and loveliest lady in the whole world. I didn't expect that she had been perfect all her life, but I seemed to think she was pretty close.

And when I asked her to open up to me about her past, she seemed to confirm that view I had of her. I had never loved anyone before like I loved your mother. I had never had those kinds of feelings in my heart for another person.

In my mind, she was the greatest thing ever, and I basically adored her. I hate to say this, but as I'm speaking now, I might have even idolized her a little bit. She seemed to me to have such a good and pure heart. Maybe I expected too much of her.

When I realized she had lied to me, it crushed me. I have never felt pain like that in my entire life. I didn't know how to deal with it. I tried to keep going in the relationship, but it seemed that I could not heal from the pain, bitterness, and betrayal that I felt.

Plus, she still wasn't being honest. She still wasn't saying anything, and that made things worse. Even after we saw those men in the restaurant, she still didn't open up to me. Each day after that felt like a new betrayal.

I had told her early on that we should share these things. I told her I had not been perfect and explained that it was safe to talk to me about her past. I thought that was necessary for a healthy relationship so that there were no surprises later on.

But when I found out that she had not told me the truth, it made me wonder if I even knew this person at all.

There were just so many things, so many voices coming at me, and so many thoughts in my mind. I didn't know what to do. It felt like there was no hope for the situation...no hope for our marriage.

But I knew it wasn't your fault. You were just caught in the middle of a bad situation. So I decided to take financial and emotional responsibility and raise you alongside her, even though we would not be together.

There was a long pause. Then Ananie asked, "But Dad, we are supposed to be Christians, right?"

"Yes, what do you mean by that?" Daniel asked.

"Well, I mean...Jesus...I mean, God the Father, He looked down on the world and He saw that we were very sinful, right?"

"Yes," Daniel replied.

"And I was recently reading in the Book of Hosea. It's like a picture of how humankind has been toward God," Ananie said.

"How do you mean?" said Daniel.

"Well, the Bible says that all have sinned and fallen short of the glory of God. The account of Hosea gives us a picture of what it feels like for God to love us and pursue us in spite of our sinfulness. You see, Hosea is a prophet of God. He is a godly man. But the Lord tells him to marry a prostitute."

"What?!" exclaimed Daniel, I'm familiar with the story of Hosea, but what does this have to do with me? Ananie then went into a lengthy explanation:

Yes. God is painting a picture of what it has been like for Him to love Israel in spite of their sinfulness and idolatry. He tells Hosea to marry a prostitute and have children with her. Hosea does this and loves her dearly. But no matter how good he is to her, she keeps running back out to adultery and prostitution.

God is showing us what it has been like for Him to love all of us. The Bible says that God demonstrates His own love for us in that while we were still sinners, Christ died for us. We were in rebellion to Him, and He sent His only Son to die for us. He did not love us because we loved Him first.

He did not love us because we were good.

He just loved us.

It's the same with Hosea and Gomer. She is a prostitute. She represents humankind, all of us in our sinful state. She did not deserve a godly husband. But Hosea, who is a metaphor for the Lord in this story, comes along and loves her anyway.

And no matter how many times she messes up, no matter how many times she hurts him, he just keeps loving her. Subsequently, every time we have an impure thought, every time we are unloving, we aren't gentle, we are mean or harsh, we give in to greed, pride, or self-righteousness, every time we fall short of His kindness, goodness, and mercy, we are like Gomer. We hurt His heart.

But He just keeps right on loving us and forgiving us. He probably has to forgive us many times each day.

As God paints this picture, this is what He says in the New International Version of Hosea 2:14-20 about the Israelites who have committed adultery by giving into idols:

Therefore I am now going to allure her;
I will lead her into the wilderness
and speak tenderly to her.
There I will give her back her vineyards,
and will make the Valley of Achor a door of hope.
There she will respond as in the days of her youth,
as in the day she came up out of Egypt.

"In that day," declares the Lord,
"you will call me 'my husband';
you will no longer call me 'my master.
I will remove the names of the Baals from her lips;
no longer will their names be invoked.
In that day I will make a covenant for them
with the beasts of the field, the birds in the sky
and the creatures that move along the ground.
Bow and sword and battle
I will abolish from the land,
so that all may lie down in safety.
I will betroth you to me forever;
I will betroth you in righteousness and justice,
in love and compassion.

I will betroth you in faithfulness,
and you will acknowledge the Lord.

The Lord says that He will come back and love us sinful human beings and treat us tenderly, even after we fall short, even after we stray from Him. After the Lord reveals this to Hosea, He then tells Hosea to go and do the same with Gomer in Hosea 3:1:

The Lord said to me, "Go, show your love to your wife again, though she is loved by another man and is an adulteress. Love her as the Lord loves the Israelites, though they turn to other gods and love the sacred raisin cakes."

So when God sent His Son to die for humankind—for you and me—He was giving us the most precious gift He could possibly give, even though we were in rebellion to Him, even though we were sinners, had betrayed Him, lied, and committed adultery with idols.

He came and pursued us and spoke tenderly to us and restored us as though nothing had ever happened.

By the way, Dad, did you know that the reason Mom didn't want to tell you the truth was only that she was afraid of losing you? It was wrong, yes, but she loved you so much that she couldn't stand the thought of losing you. As a result, she made a mistake. She still loves you, and she regrets everything.

At that point, Daniel could not take any more of the grief in his heart. He cried out right there in the middle of the park, "Lord, please forgive my unforgiveness, and heal my broken heart. The betrayal hurt me so bad, Lord, that I just didn't know what to do. I'm sorry for holding Jackie's mistakes against her all of these years. Please remove bitterness, resentment, and pride from my heart. Heal us and make our family whole again."

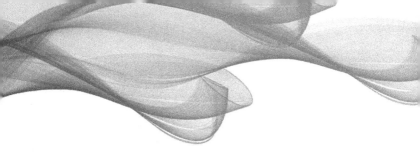

Chapter 10

A Changed Heart

*M*aking their way to the nearest park bench, Ananie gently extended her hand toward her father. She could tell that he was quite distraught after revealing his heart, but she prayed that he would be set free and her parents' marriage would be restored. Satan had already stolen way too much from her family. Yet this time, something in the atmosphere began to change. Daniel wiped the flowing tears from his cheeks, and Ananie hugged him. Then he confessed that it was time.

"Time for what?" sweet Ananie questioned, gently letting go of her tight grasp and inching closer to her dad.

"Time for me to let go of the past with your mom and allow God to bring healing," Daniel explained anxiously.

"What do you mean exactly, Dad? You've already asked Jesus for forgiveness, and He forgives you!" Ananie gleamed.

"I mean, my precious daughter, that it is time I take back what Satan has stolen from our marriage, from our family. He stole sexual intimacy, purity, trust, and forgiveness. He stole our marriage and broke our family, and I let him do it," Daniel replied in a soft tone.

"It's time for me to acknowledge that I, too, am a sinner, that Jesus died for me on the cross, and that your mother needs forgiveness just like I need forgiveness from the Lord daily. I've treated her like her sins were unforgivable. Oh, Ananie," Daniel began to cry. "I am wrong for how I've treated your mom. Her lying to me wasn't right, but me holding it against her all these years wasn't right either. I turned cold, stubborn, and foolish, refusing to forgive her. I don't know how she could ever forgive me, how she could ever forget the look I gave her when I told her I had filed for divorce, and the heartbreak I saw in her eyes the night we said goodbye." Daniel shook his head as tears flowed in a heavy stream from his eyes down to the park bench. He bent slightly, placing his hands over his eyes so that his elbows rested on his knees as he wept. Ananie comforted her father to the best of her ability and placed her hands on his back as she began to pray out loud for her father.

"Dear God," Ananie began, before erupting into a prayer that was guided by the Holy Spirit. "I just want to lift up my dad, Daniel, right here and right now to you. Lord, you see the brokenness in his heart, but he is repentant, Father, and asks You to redeem and restore this situation. We ask, Lord, that a flood of forgiveness will sweep into this situation. That it will take over the space that lies between Dad and Mom until so much love and restoration exist it's inevitable to feel anything else. I pray, Father, that in Your powerful name, the broken be made whole, and these hurts will be healed. That even in their pain, Your love will begin to patch and soothe, bringing them together, and home yet again. That, like Hosea, Lord, You will lead Dad to a place of forgiveness, acceptance, and unconditional love. Satan has stolen way too much from them, from our family, from me, as I watched their fragmented love all these years. But, You, Jesus, You're stronger than all of these things. As Scripture tells us, the thief only comes to steal, kill, and destroy, but, You, Lord, You come to bring us life and life to the fullest. Let that be true for my parents. Allow Mom to forgive Dad and confess and repent of her own sins. Let Dad extend Your unconditional love to her. And God, we ask that You rejoin together what no man, or even the devil, can separate. In Jesus' name, I pray. Amen."

Hugging again on the park bench, Daniel thanked his daughter for praying such a beautiful prayer for him and Jackie. He was so proud of the woman she was becoming at just eighteen years old. And as something began to stir in his own heart, he knew that Ananie was right. This work of destruction between him and Jackie was never what the Lord intended. All this time, all these years, they'd been fighting a fight they were never meant to battle. How had he been so blind? After all, their battles were not against flesh and blood, but rulers and principalities of the evil one. But it wasn't too late. God could restore their marriage, even now, in their brokenness and suffering.

Quickly taking his daughter's hand, Daniel said that he needed to talk to Jackie at that moment; if it weren't done within the next few hours, he'd never gain the courage to confess his own fault of unforgiveness. Though his body now shook with nervousness and fear, he truly believed the Lord could make all things new—even the fragmented love he'd lost with his beautiful wife.

Making their way to the fifth house on Cain Creek Trail, Daniel felt an odd yet familiar nostalgia when he and Jackie first fell in love, when they first bought this home and were expecting little Ananie, now some eighteen years ago.

He reminisced over the good times—the seconds, minutes, hours, days, months, and years—they'd had in that place. The kiss they shared by the front door. The way Jackie looked when she was excited to share news with him.

Quickly jumping out of the car, Ananie watched her father race up to the steps of the front door, only to stop short just a few feet from its frame. Sheepishly backing away, he slowly stepped back until he was even with the pavement and then sat with his legs crossed on the ground. Watching his facial expressions from a distance, she could tell her father was distraught. He was in agony like a man too broken to know what to do next.

Then all of a sudden, he did something surprising. He stood up, lifted his hands to the heavens, and prayed. And as he prayed, his frame began to relax. His posture melted in the presence of God, who had the ability to restore him. At that moment, Ananie knew her father was healed.

Racing back to the door, Daniel knocked on the exterior wood frame. Ananie, who still sat watching from the car, got out, shut the door, and followed her father's footsteps.

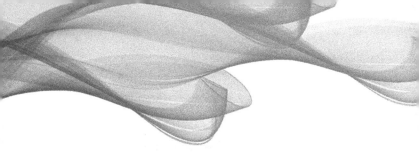

Chapter 11

Reconciliation and Restoration

"Daniel?" Jackie questioned. "Why are you and Ananie back so early? Is something wrong? You weren't supposed to be back till this evening. Is she okay?" Her eyes darted anxiously between Daniel and Ananie.

"Oh yes, Jackie," Daniel affirmed. "Ananie is great, but I really need to talk with you."

Jackie noticed the hesitation in his eyes. She feared he wasn't telling her everything—that there was something wrong. Then all of a sudden, seemingly out of the blue, her mind flashed to that dreaded night when they lost their love, the night she cried herself to sleep because the pain was just too much, when she wondered if he had ever really loved her. Because if he did, why would he leave?

"Jackie?" Daniel asked again, waving his loose fingers in front of her eyes. "We lost you for a second. Are you okay?" Daniel pondered, looking very tender and earnest toward her, a look she had not seen in quite a while, a look Jackie recognized from when they were first courting.

"Yeah, I'm fine." Jackie reaffirmed, snapping herself out of the memory, throwing it away like the other thoughts she tried to burn away in her mind. "What did you need to talk about?" she inquired, welcoming Daniel into the living room. He took a seat beside her on the couch while Ananie quickly scurried up to her room so her parents could talk.

Sitting beside her on the couch, Daniel knew it was time. Heart pounding, mind racing, and limbs clammy, he began his address full speed before Satan could try to talk him out of it:

Jackie, here's the thing. Sixteen years ago, I lost something that I never thought I'd lose. I lost true, pure, and lifelong love that I was thankful to the Lord for blessing me with. I remember when we first met, Jackie, how in love with you I was from the time we first began dating, how the Lord was leading me to you, and as a young man in college, I felt so nervous. I felt like I was going to mess it up. You seemed so perfect, so out of my league. When we started courting, I couldn't believe someone as beautiful as you would even give me a chance.

That day I asked you about your past I knew the frailty and fallenness of my own past. I knew my sins had etched my soul with stains that I couldn't remove on my own. I didn't want you to know my past, but I knew that in sharing our vulnerabilities, the Lord would bless us. So when you told me about your sexual history, I believed you, but I still wanted you.

Jackie, I wanted to be with you more than anything else in this world. And though it was wrong, I realize that now I was expecting something that wasn't even realistic. I was holding up a sacred ideal of perfection in the marriage relationship, one that meant we would somehow never deeply hurt or betray each other. In truth, human beings make mistakes. We do hurt each other sometimes, and God tells us to forgive each other when that happens. He doesn't say to expect that it will never happen.

For my own unforgiveness, I have since asked God for forgiveness. I am now asking you. But my sweet love, there is something even greater I need your forgiveness for, and that takes me back to that night after the restaurant incident.

I remember going to the bathroom and seeing your old lovers that you never told me about. I recall them scoffing you and saying vulgar things about you, and I couldn't believe it. Though I wanted to shake their words from my mind, it was too late. The truth of their accusations was confirmed to me when I came back and saw the look of fear and shame on your face. I didn't have to ask because I knew deep in my heart that something was wrong.

And in all honesty, my selfish pride thought it was you. I felt like I couldn't trust you because you'd lied. But the truth was that I had placed a standard of perfect honesty on you. I expected that you would never tell me a lie under any circumstance.

No human being can live up to a standard of perfection, so when this flawless image came crashing down, I left the problem behind. The catch was, I, too, was the problem because I had made unrealistic expectations you could never uphold. I treated you like your sin was the worst sin in the world. But in reality, I, too, am imperfect.

I may not have lied about my past, but I sometimes let anger get the best of me. I sometimes treated you harshly. I was guilty of being judgmental and unforgiving. I am sometimes impatient. I can be prideful and self-righteous sometimes. I have my own sins, weaknesses, and shortcomings, and I need forgiveness daily.

God has revealed these truths to my heart, Jackie, and I am so sorry. That day, the day we said goodbye, I feel like I lost my world. I lost the good gift God had given me because I was too selfish and prideful to realize that, in God's eyes, all sin is wrong, and the right way to deal with it is to forgive the person. Yes, you hurt me, but I never once stopped to think about how I hurt you. I loved you then and I love you now, Jackie.

Glancing up to pause, Daniel hadn't realized that Jackie was quietly weeping, lifting her hands in prayer to the Lord. "Thank you, Father," he saw Jackie mouth as she caught his eyes looking at her and then tried to recompose herself quickly.

"Oh, Daniel," Jackie started. "I've been praying for years for this moment," she noted, wiping the tears from her eyes. "I just never thought it would happen. Many years ago, I used to read the story of Hosea and Gomer from the Bible, and I would ask God to give you forgiveness and love like Hosea had for Gomer. It has been so long that I had given up hope that this would ever truly happen. But now, here you are, telling me you love me and asking for forgiveness. God, I praise You and thank You!"

"Jackie," Daniel soothed, reaching his hand out to hers.

"No, it's okay," she reaffirmed. "Let me finish. I want you to know that not only do I forgive you, but it's my prayer you will forgive me too. What I did, not telling you the truth, was completely wrong, and it cost us our marriage. I know we both said things we didn't mean, but it doesn't matter anymore. Jesus washed it all in His blood a long time ago. We are clean in His sight, and He has made our relationship clean again too."

"Jackie," Daniel started again. "You won't believe this, but Ananie used the illustration of Hosea with me, and it was their story that the Holy Spirit used to convict my heart just a little while ago."

A smile crossed Jackie's face. "That girl," Jackie retorted. "We've been doing a mother-daughter Bible study for weeks, and she kept saying God wanted us to study the Book of Hosea," Jackie shook her head and laughed.

"I guess God knew what He was doing," Daniel chimed in.

"I guess He did," Jackie agreed, nodding her head and leaning it against Daniel ever so slightly.

"So, what does that mean for us?" Daniel questioned, his eyes glimmering.

But just as Jackie was about to answer, they heard a loud thud. Rushing to the staircase just around the corner, Daniel and Jackie laughed at their still childish daughter who had camped out on the stairs to listen to their conversation, only to get too close and slide down the last few steps to the bottom of the floor.

"What in the world were you doing, Ananie?" Jackie demanded gently.

"Well, I just had to know that you and Dad were going to be okay!" Ananie innocently remarked as a sheepish grin crossed her face.

"I suppose that's a valid excuse, my dear. It's apparent now that God was working through you to help your father and me," Jackie replied.

"Really?" Ananie jumped with excitement.

"Really," Daniel and Jackie confirmed, shocking themselves as they spoke in unison.

Looking at one another, Ananie knew her parents were falling in love again. She knew that this was the moment she'd prayed for. Pushing them both back into the living room, she raced up the stairs only to come back down and take up her spot again on the stairs.

"That silly girl," Daniel laughed. "She's definitely your daughter," he confirmed.

"Hey, now," Jackie playfully nudged his side. "It takes two to tango," she flirted, then anxiously apologized if that was too forward.

"Honestly," Daniel began, "I waited my whole life to find the one my soul could love, and I still believe you're that woman. Yes, we've both made mistakes. Yes, we're both sinful. And yes, we allowed Satan to enter and destroy our marriage through sin, but it doesn't have to stay that way. God can redeem us like Hosea and Gomer, Jackie. If He loved humankind enough to demonstrate His love to a sinful nation, to love like Hosea loved Gomer, He surely loves you and me enough to restore our marriage."

"But Daniel," Jackie spoke cautiously, removing her hand from his. "We aren't kids anymore. This isn't some love story fairytale. It's real life, with real problems and real issues. I forgive you, and you forgive me, but how would that ever be enough to restore us?" she questioned, as tears again began to well up in her eyes.

"Well," Daniel pondered, clearing his throat a few times for good measure. "Here's the thing. On our own, we will never be good enough. You know that. Our sin, my sin, your sin, the sin of the world separates us from God. We allowed Satan and sin to rob us of way more than we ever bargained for.

"But God? He still loves us. He fights for us daily. He wants us, His children, to be in fellowship and communion with Him. So that marriage Satan stole? It can be redeemed. The sexual impurity that has haunted us both, God sees no more. He loves you, Jackie, and He loves me. And Jackie, as much as it scares me to say this, I love you. God is far greater than our highs and lows, and if you're willing, I'm willing to work for restoration. Not just for a month, an hour, or a day, but for the rest of our lives. Are you?"

His questions caught her off guard. How could he know that she'd never stopped loving him? How could they make this work? How was God going to restore this? But in the darkness of fear and doubt, light began to break through. She began to see that their own marriage could be an illustration of God's love and redemption. Though the sin was oh so costly, Jesus paid for it all when He died on the cross for her, for Daniel, for all. Why should she live like that wasn't true?

"Oh, Daniel," Jackie cried out, standing up as she began to pace the oak floor. "Eighteen years ago, I gave you my heart, and it ended up shattered. I felt bruised and broken. I knew it was wrong that I'd lied to you, but I was honestly just afraid I was going to lose you. It was wrong, and I should've told you, but since that day, the day you left me, I never stopped loving you.

"I never stopped praying for you and hoping our marriage could be restored. I just can't believe it's happening, so it scares me. It scares me silly to think this isn't a dream, or that it isn't all going to crumble away tomorrow. I've craved love for such a long time that it has made life very hard through the years.

"I've cried on the floor just wanting to experience love. But you know what? In those times, God was always close to me. He spoke to my heart. He gave me closeness and intimacy with Him, which was far greater than any human love, and I truly believe He has done a restorative act in me because the truth is, Daniel, what man intended for evil, God can still use for good. Our relationship hasn't been stolen, it's just been on a sabbatical. God can restore. It's time to take back what belongs to us, His children."

With love in his eyes, Daniel stood up, gently extended a hand to Jackie, and pulled her close like they were young again. Peering from the corner, Ananie watched them embrace passionately, like two sinners being set free from their chains.

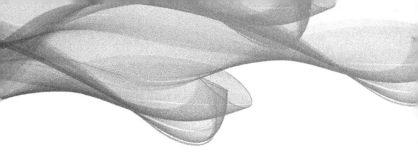

Conclusion

Parting Words for Parents

*F*irst, I want to say thank you! Thank you for taking some of your very important time to read this book. My hope is that you can personally relate to some of the fictional illustrations in this book.

Second, I hope that this book encourages you, parents, to sit down with your children and teens and communicate about these issues. If you made mistakes in your past, pray about sharing some with your children. Explain the repercussions and the valuable lessons you have learned. Just like Solomon did with his son in the Book of Proverbs, implore your children to get wisdom and understanding.

Third, please know that there is grace for you. Wherever you have messed up, there is forgiveness. And wherever there is brokenness or loss, there is an opportunity for healing and restoration. Sin can be very costly. It can often bring years of unnecessary pain and heartbreak into lives and families. But our God is a God of healing and restoration.

Last, if you need to forgive someone, ask God for the power to do it. He will answer that prayer 100 percent of the time.

Do these things and you can stand tall and proudly say, "I'm building up a strong foundation."

Parting Words for Young Women

Young women, you are valuable in the eyes of God. You are valuable in the eyes of the right young man. Be valuable in your own eyes.

Muhammad Ali is said to have once reacted to his daughter wearing revealing clothing by explaining to her that everything God made valuable, such as gold, diamonds, and other precious stones, was way down in the earth, covered up, and protected. He then reportedly said, "Your body is sacred. You're far more precious than diamonds and pearls, and you should be covered too."

This is sound advice.

May God bless you all throughout your life as you love Him, pursue Him, and walk in His ways. He loves you, and He only wants the best for you!

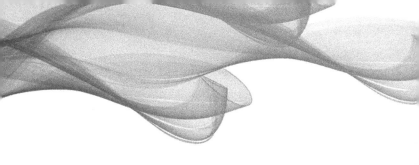

About the Author

*J*ean Marie Désir was born in Port-au-Prince, Haiti, in a Christian family. He is the second-born among seven children, and he began singing for the Lord in his adolescent years at his local church in Pétion-Ville, Haiti. At the age of ten, he realized he truly had a passion to sing for the glory of God, with whom he began to build a long-lasting relationship.

He attended high school at Lycée de Pétion-Ville. He studied Management at L'Institut Superieur de Biblioeconomie et de Gestion and later moved to Miami, FL, where he earned a degree in computer business application.

Jean Marie Désir has been with numerous groups; many of which he founded and led, such as: Les Enfants bénis de Jesus, Eldaa, Resistance, Fusion, Les Sardonyx de Miami, and Constellation with Assad Francoeur. As his ministry grows, he's been able to testify of the presence and glory of the Lord during these experiences.

In October 1999, Jean Marie Désir moved from Florida to Atlanta, GA, where he earned a double major in science in business and accounting, and also began his solo singing ministry. He has sought to bring others to Christ through his unique voice and untouchable lyrics.

In the spring of 2003, Jean Marie Désir released the long-awaited solo album, *He's Alive*, and after three years of hiatus, by popular demand, Jean Marie launched his second album in Creole, French, and English, entitled, *Jericho*. Désir has been busy ministering and performing his anointed music on the road. As a vocalist, songwriter, composer, producer, and performer, Désir garnered the respect of his peers within the Christian industry. His insightful use of words, accompanied by an ability to convey the message, has lured the attention of even non-Christians.

Boasting of a sound that is unique and yet universal, Desir's music appeals to people of all ages, backgrounds, and styles. The *Jericho* project is an uplifting presentation, which takes you through many moods and feelings. The album is not just a listening experience but a journey of worship. It will take you on a journey into the Holy Place and draw you to seek God's face.

When asked what stirs him to sing or perform, he is quick to respond, "God alone is the reason for the zeal exhibited in my life. My songs are songs of the heart and simple intimate expressions of prophetic worship. I love to worship! We were created to do nothing but worship God! There is nothing more powerful than a man worshiping God. My success is in God and in Him being pleased with my life." When you meet Jean Marie Désir, you will not only meet a singer, an author, a composer, an arranger, a promoter, a husband, a father, and a servant of God, but a new friend who is full of life, with a contagious love for God, church, and family.

Discography

1997:Fax Machine, Mini Records.

1999: Mwen Vle Ale, Les Sardonyx.

2003: He's Alive, Glorious Sounds Productions.

2007: Jericho, Glorious Sounds Productions.

Recognition/Honors:

1999: Award of Merit; by Les Sardonyx, Acapella of Miami, FL

2000: Artist of the Year; by Open Bible Church Tabernacle, Marietta, GA.

2001: Artist of the Year; by Ebenezer S.D.A. Church, Atlanta, GA.

2001: Award of Recognition for Haitian Christian Artists.

2004: Artist of the Year; by MichManou Ministries.

2007: Award of Merit; by Maranatha Christ Revient Ministry.

2008: Award of Merit; by Atlanta Haitian Church of God.

2011: Award of Merit; by OHAHIM Annual Youth Talents Show. (just to name a few).

Guest Appearances

Trinity Broadcasting Network (T.B.N.).

Haitian Television Network (H.T.N).

Christ est La Réponse (Manhattan, NY TV 26).

Le Ministère de Maranatha Christ Revient (Access TV) Chicago IL,

Radio Carnivale, And Radio Arc-en-ciel, (just to name a few).

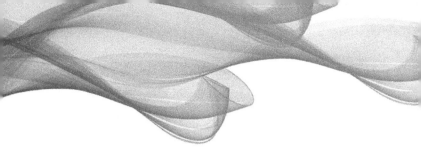

Endnotes

1   "11 Facts About High School Dropout Rates." *DoSomething.Org*, https://www.dosomething.org/us/facts/11-facts-about-high-school-dropout-rates Accessed 18 February 2020.

2   "The Greatest – Muhammed Ali's Advice to his Daughters." *myFatherdaughter*, https://myfatherdaughter.com/the-greatest-muhammed-alis-advice-to-his-daughters/ Accessed 18 February 2020

CPSIA information can be obtained
at www.ICGtesting.com
Printed in the USA
BVHW041641060421
604327BV00015B/910